Video Rivals

Sonia Sarfati

Illustrations by
Pierre Durand

Translated by
Sarah Cummins

Formac Publishing Limited
Halifax, Nova Scotia
1995

Originally published as Tricot, piano et jeu vidéo

Copyright © 1992 la courte échelle

Translation copyright © 1995 by Formac Publishing Limited

Canadian Cataloguing in Publication Data

   Sarfati, Sonia.

   [Tricot, piano et jeu vidéo. English]

   Video Rivals

   (First Novel Series)

   Translation of: Tricot, piano et jeu vidéo.

ISBN 0-88780-314-8 (paper)
ISBN 0-88780-315-6 (board)

I. Durand, Pierre, 1955- II. Title. III. Title: Tricot, piano et
jeu vidéo. English. IV. Series.

PS8587.A3767T7413 1995   jc843'.54   C95-950110-X
PZ7.S37Vi 1995

Formac Publishing Limited
5502 Atlantic Street
Halifax, N.S. B3H 1G4

Printed and bound in Canada

Table of contents

Introduction

Raphael was knitting. Knitting as his great-grandmother had done, as his grandmother had done, as his mother—well, no, not knitting as his mother had done. His mother had never knit a stitch in her life.

But Raphael was knitting. Not because he liked to knit, but because he had to knit. All because of what had happened last Thursday...

1
A new friend

Thursday afternoon, Raphael left school by himself. All the others headed off in groups, talking about their plans for the long Easter weekend, which was just beginning.

Myriam was Raphael's only friend. She was at the cottage with her parents, so Raphael had nobody to discuss his plans with. But that didn't bother him.

Oh, all right, it *did* bother him. It hurt. But he was beginning to get used to it. That's just the way things had been since he started at a new school two weeks ago.

Before that, Raphael had gone to Dominion Junior School. And ever since junior kindergarten, Raphael had reigned supreme over all of Dominion Junior School. Everyone wanted to be friends with Raphael. Why? Because Raphael could always come up with fun ideas and make up exciting stories.

Like the story of the kangaroo that got seasick whenever it jumped. Fortunately, the kangaroo met a bear that taught it how to walk.

Then Raphael moved. Now he was going to a bigger school, and he was in a new class where everyone else already knew each other.

Now, it is possible to be a lot of fun and have a great imagination and still be very shy. Raphael was like that. And that's why he hadn't made any new friends, except for Myriam.

Raphael definitely intended to make some other new friends. He had several ideas about how to go about it, but some of them were a bit too weird to actually carry out.

He could hold a pyjama party in his uncle Louis's expensive, fashionable French restaurant.

He could form a rock band called The Cave Men that would make music by banging on rocks with pickaxes, hammers and screwdrivers.

But when Raphael heard about the video game championship,

he thought, "Here's my chance! If I win, the others are bound to notice me."

Raphael didn't play with his video game very often. When he was first given it, he had a lot of fun with it. But after a couple of months, he found it boring. So he went back to his favourite pastime, writing and illustrating stories.

Raphael figured that he would have to train seriously if he intended to win the championship. And that's what he had been doing for the past week, and what he planned to do all through Easter vacation.

"Hey! Wait up!"

Raphael was surprised. He turned around and found himself face to face with Damian.

Damian was one of the most popular kids in Raphael's class, maybe in the whole school. At least he was popular with the other kids. Not so popular with the teachers.

Damian was very bossy. He lost his temper over trifles, and he only did what he was told when he felt like it. Which is to say, not very often.

Nonetheless, Damian was always surrounded by friends. That was because he had the most fabulous bike and the best video game system.

Also, his parents let him rent horror films to watch on their giant television screen, and he could invite his best friends over to watch with him.

"So, are you going to enter

the video game championship?" Damian asked Raphael.

"Uh ... yes."

"I didn't know you liked to play video games," Damian went on. "Are you any good?"

Raphael didn't know what to say. He was still surprised at how nice Damian was being to him. He opened his mouth to answer, but Damian, always in a hurry, wouldn't let him get a word in. "Want to have a game? Shall we go to your house?"

Raphael couldn't get over it. Damian was interested in him because he was entering the video game championship!

"Sure!" he cried happily. "Come on!"

2
Raphael wins ... and loses

Twenty minutes later, the two boys were sitting in front of Raphael's television screen beginning their game.

Smash! An airplane crashes. Yikes! A vampire crawls out! Quick, get a cross to chase it away. There! Whew!

Another rumble in the sky! What is it, another airplane? No, it's a dragon! Get the knight with his magic armour. The dragon starts spitting fire, and...

And Raphael wins the game!

Damian frowned, more in puzzlement than anger. Raphael

beamed. He never realized he was that good!

"Let's have another game," said Damian curtly.

Raphael was so happy that Damian wanted to stay and play that he never noticed his new friend was now in a bad mood. He threw himself enthusiastically into a new game and started to rack up points.

"Hold on!" cried Damian, suddenly. He was losing again. "I'm thirsty."

Raphael was a bit surprised, but he stopped playing and went to get something to drink. He was upstairs in the kitchen when he heard a loud yell.

"What's the matter?" he asked, running back downstairs.

Damian had a strange look on his face, nervous and annoyed at the same time.

"Your video game doesn't work any more!" he exclaimed after a few seconds.

Raphael opened his mouth, but no sound came out.

"You're kidding, aren't you?" he said, finally.

But he could see that Damian wasn't joking. When he pressed the buttons on the control pad, nothing happened.

"Did you take out the cartridge?" he asked hopefully.

"No, no!" stammered Damian. "Anyway, the player is stuck. I couldn't eject the cartridge to figure out what the problem is. Uh, sorry. I have to go now!"

Clutching his broken video game, Raphael watched Damian go upstairs. In a few seconds he heard the kitchen door slam.

And Raphael was alone. Again.

3
Video training

Raphael was sure of one thing: he had to keep on training, even if his video game was broken. And he couldn't get it fixed before Tuesday because the shops were closed for the Easter holiday.

Raphael had to figure out a new way to exercise his fingers. That's right. Runners have to strengthen their legs. Singers have to train their voice. To win at video games, you have to get your fingers in shape.

For the rest of the afternoon he thought about training, and all through the evening. All night long ... well, actually not all night long. Problems or no problems, Raphael always dropped off to sleep very quickly.

The next morning, he woke up with a start. An idea had just occurred to him. The piano! All he had to do was play the piano! That would keep his fingers moving!

The only problem was that Raphael had never taken any music lessons. But not to worry, he could improvise.

A great idea, wasn't it? Probably it was. But not at eight o'clock in the morning, on a holiday Friday ... when your parents are still sleeping.

"What the heck is going on?" cried Raphael's dad, running into the living room with

Raphael's mom when the concert was under way.

"Oops," Raphael said to himself. "I forgot."

Fortunately, he managed to extricate himself from a sticky situation, as usual, by acting like a goof. He stood up suddenly, closed his eyes, stretched his arms out in front of him, and started to walk and snore at the same time.

He could hear his parents sniggering behind his back.

"Hey, sleepwalker!" called his mother. "Be a nice guy and give Sarah her breakfast."

Sarah was Raphael's six-year-old sister. After breakfast, they went outside, and a new idea came to Raphael as he watched her.

"Sarah, would you like to be a princess with incredible powers? You know, in a country far, far away, the kings and the queens make lots of braids in their hair. And the more braids they have, the more powerful they are."

That was all it took to convince Sarah. She sat down in

front of Raphael, and let him make one braid, two braids, ten, twenty-one, forty-six braids in her hair!

For an hour he was able to exercise his fingers as he told Sarah stories to keep her still while he went on braiding. But after a while, there was no more hair left to braid on the princess's head.

"Uh, let's see," he said. "Some of these braids are crooked. I'll undo them and braid them over again."

But Sarah decided she had better things to do than let her brother fool around with her hair all day long!

So Raphael went back up to his room. He braided the hair on two Indian dolls his parents had brought back from a trip. They looked very handsome with this new hairstyle.

Then he put braids on a few of his stuffed animals. It made his angora cat and his hairy monster look like hedgehogs, with little braids sticking up all over their body!

Then Raphael tried to braid the fur on Taxi, his big white and grey dog. However, Taxi did not appreciate this treatment. She grew restless after a few seconds and ran away.

There was nothing left to braid in the whole house, except for his mom's and dad's hair. Somehow Raphael didn't think his parents would agree to it.

Finally, in the middle of the afternoon, he discovered the

solution to his problem.

When he got back from taking Taxi for a walk in the park, he found his grandmother had come for a visit.

She was sitting in the living room listening to music, tapping out the beat with her foot. Not with her hands. They were far too busy with her knitting.

What was fascinating to Raphael was how fast her hands were moving.

In a flash, Raphael was seated on the couch, holding a knitting needle in each hand. His grandmother, somewhat astonished, was teaching him to knit. She even gave him his own ball of wool.

"Now you can make a nice scarf," she said.

4
Damian's betrayal

So that was why Raphael had been knitting for the past three days. He had produced a long red strip that resembled a scarf...very slightly.

He was sitting in the living room, his knitting in his lap, when the front door opened.

"Hello, everybody!"

Raphael looked up. It was Charlie! His aunt Charlie. Her real name was Charlotte...and she was an electronics technician! Why hadn't he thought of her earlier, to fix his video game?

"Yippee!" he yelled.

He threw himself into her arms. She burst out laughing.

"What a welcome, Raphael! I bet you need me for something."

Charlie was just teasing. Raphael was always very happy to see his aunt. But today, it was true, he did need her for something. He explained what the problem was, and a screwdriver appeared, as if by magic, in Charlie's hand.

"I will see the patient now!"

In a trice, she had opened up the system. "What the—?" she muttered, wrinkling her nose.

"What is this stuff?" she exclaimed, looking at her sticky fingers.

"What's wrong?" asked

Raphael. "Is it something serious?"

"No, but it sure is strange. Can you explain to me why there is a coin blocking the game? And why is this thing full of chewing gum?"

Raphael's eyes widened. Chewing gum? Chewing gum! Yes indeed, he could explain

why there was chewing gum in his cartridge player. There was a certain person in his class at school who always has a wad of chewing gum in his mouth—Damian.

When he had come over to Raphael's house, he had been chewing three or four pieces of gum, as usual. And now, thinking it over, Raphael was sure that Damian hadn't been chewing anything when he left.

"Can you fix it?" he asked, trying to hide his anger and disappointment.

"Sure, no problem!" answered Charlie.

Three-quarters of an hour later, the video game was working again. Delighted, Raphael hugged his aunt.

But his happiness was short-lived. Yes, the video game was working well. Extremely well. Perfectly well.

However, despite all his piano playing, braiding, and knitting, Raphael's scores were not as high as the scores he had reached last week.

It figured. The fingers that get the most use when you're playing a video game are the thumbs. But you use your thumbs very little when you knit.

It was all Damian's fault. "I'll get even," vowed Raphael.

5
Revenge

"Hi, Raph!"

Raphael jumped. He was so lost in his plans for vengeance that he hadn't noticed when someone came into the playroom.

"Myriam! You're back from the country!"

"Yes," answered his friend. "Steve had to come back early. He's going to a big party this evening."

Steve was Myriam's older brother. He was 17. This year he had made some new friends, and Myriam reported that he was turning into a bit of a hood-lum.

Raphael wasn't quite sure what she meant by that. He did know that he always felt very uncomfortable around Steve.

"Want to have a game?" asked Myriam, pointing to the video system.

"Okay," Raphael answered.

But after a few minutes of play, Myriam stopped and stared at her pal.

"You're missing easy shots! If you don't feel like playing, just say so. I'll go have a game with Steve."

Raphael was about to protest when he suddenly thought of something. Steve! Steve was a bit of a hoodlum....

"Is he at home?" he cried.

Myriam nodded.

"I have to talk to him."

"To who? Steve?" Myriam was astonished.

"Uh ... he's taken courses in electronics, hasn't he?" said Raphael. "Maybe he can help me figure out what's wrong with my parents' computer."

"Oh, I see...okay, let's go."

A few minutes later, Raphael got to Myriam's house. He went into the garage where Steve was fixing his motorcycle.

"Ahem!" he coughed, to catch Steve's attention.

"Who is it?" muttered Steve, looking up with a worried expression. When he saw it was Raphael, he seemed relieved.

"Oh, it's you! What do you want?"

Raphael swallowed hard.

"I ... I ... I need you to carry out a mission," he said weakly.

Steve burst out laughing.

"I need you to carry out a mission," he repeated in a deep voice. "On this TV program I used to watch when I was your age, the chief was always saying

that to his men."

Then he turned serious.

"So, you need me to carry out a mission?"

Although he was feeling more nervous than ever, Raphael decided to carry through with his plan. He nodded.

"Yes," he whispered. "I want you to steal Damian's video game."

6
Confiscated!

The next day, vacation was over. Raphael dragged his feet all the way to school. His head was full of dark ideas.

Dark ideas that grew even darker as he passed by Damian's house. There was his rival sitting on the stairs, his elbows on his knees and his hands over his face.

"What's up?" asked Raphael, curiously.

Damian lifted his head. His eyes were red.

"Oh, it's you!" he shouted. "Go away. Don't bug me."

"But ... I ... what's happened?" asked Raphael, turning pale.

"There was a storm! You know what a storm is, don't you? Well, there was a storm last night!" cried Damian.

"Yeah, so what?" asked Raphael, who still didn't know what was going on.

"You want to know the whole story?" Damian yelled even louder. "Just so you can make fun of me. Well, I'll tell you. And then you can go and tell everybody else. And maybe you'll all die laughing!"

In a furious voice, Damian told how he had been wakened by the storm in the middle of the night, and had turned on his video game. But his dad woke

up too and came in and found him playing, and his dad had confiscated his system for two weeks!

So that was all! Raphael was relieved and started to laugh.

Damian, enraged, bounded down the steps and ran off towards the school. He didn't even hear what Raphael called after him.

"Hey, you know, I can teach you how to knit. It's very handy, when you can't play with your video games!"

Raphael was still laughing when he heard the sound of a motor behind him. Then a horn beeped. He turned around. There was Steve on his motorcycle.

7
The word from Steve

Steve's hands were sheathed in black leather gloves. He lifted one hand, pointed a finger at Raphael, and beckoned him to come closer.

Suddenly Raphael didn't feel like laughing any more.

"Hi, Raph!" a clear voice piped up.

It was Myriam! Raphael hadn't even seen her sitting on the motorcycle behind her big brother. She looked funny, with a huge helmet on her head.

"Hi," Raphael finally found the nerve to say.

"Steve is taking me to school on his motorbike," said Myriam.

"That's ... that's nice," Raphael answered, keeping his eyes downcast.

"Hey you!"

Raphael swallowed hard, and took a deep breath.

"Yes?"

Steve burst out laughing.

"Cat got your tongue? Seems to me you weren't so shy yesterday. Say, little sister, I hope your friend is usually more talkative than he is now!"

Myriam seemed surprised. Raphael had really been acting strange since yesterday.

"What's wrong, Raph?" she asked.

Raphael opened his mouth to reply, but Steve cut him off.

"I know what's wrong with him! He came to talk to me yesterday and, without meaning to, he told me something that he had been asked not to repeat."

Hearing the story that Steve was making up, Raphael blushed. He could see himself standing in the garage yesterday and asking Steve to steal Damian's video game. And Steve laughing his head off, laughing so hard he couldn't stop.

Ashamed, Raphael had run off. And now hearing Steve, he felt like running away again.

"Now," said Steve, "I think he's afraid I'm going to blab his story around to everyone. That's why he looks like he doesn't know where to hide. But I can keep a secret, you know."

As he spoke, he removed something from one of the pockets of his leather jacket.

"You left in such a hurry yesterday," he said, handing an envelope to Raphael. "I think you dropped this."

And before anyone could say another word, he kickstarted his motorcycle and cried, "Hold on, little sister! We're off!"

Raphael was left alone on the sidewalk. In his hands, he held a white envelope, stained with grease. With beating heart he opened it. There was a piece of paper inside.

Do you really think burglary is a good idea? I'm sure that now you've thought it over, you've changed your mind.

Myriam told me that you're a smart kid. So I'm sure you'll find another way to solve your problem! And since I have a very poor memory, I can tell you I've already forgotten what you told me.

So long!

Raphael sighed in relief. Steve was right, he knew. He had known it ever since he had stupidly uttered the sentence: "I want you to steal Damian's video game."

There was a big difference between imagining such terrible things and actually doing them. How could he have ever entertained such a crazy idea?

Raphael now felt lighthearted. Everything was back to normal. Or almost everything. There was still the championship.

8
Damian versus Raphael?

The great day finally arrived. All the kids in the neighbourhood who wanted to enter the competition were filing into the school where the championship matches were to take place.

Raphael stood in line-up right behind Damian.

"Stop staring at my back, you're bugging me!" snapped Damian.

"Tough!" retorted Raphael.

Damian turned around, his eyes flashing.

"You, you little..."

Fortunately, a monitor came

up. "Cut it out, you two. Under-
stand?"

At that moment, the line
started to move forward. Soon
Damian had reached the table
where a girl, Catherine, was
signing in the contestants.

"Your name and date of birth,
please."

Damian told her.

"Hey! It was your birthday
last week!" exclaimed Catherine. "I hope that will bring you
good luck!"

"What a baby!" thought Damian.

"Go down the hall to your left," Catherine instructed him.

"I'll wait for my...friend," said Damian. "We'll go together."

Catherine turned to Raphael, filled out his entry form, and told him to go down the hall to his right!

"How come he's supposed to go to the right?" demanded Damian. "We want to be together!"

"You can't," explained Catherine. "You just turned ten. You're now in the category for ten and eleven-year-olds. Raphael is still in the category of eight and nine-year-olds."

"Does that mean we won't

play against each other?" asked Damian, his voice shaking with rage.

"That's right. Maybe next year you will."

Damian clenched his fists.

Raphael was disappointed. He would have like to prove his superiority over Damian. And show him that it had been totally useless to sabotage his video game.

Conclusion

Four hours later, the results of the championship were announced.

Damian had finished in third place in his category. He looked furious.

Raphael had finished second among the eight- and nine-year-olds. He smiled, pleased that he had done better than Damian, even if they weren't in the same category.

But there was another reason for him to be happy. The person who had come in first among the eight- and nine-year-olds

was ... Myriam.

Of course, she had a very good coach: a fellow named Steve.

It should also be mentioned

that she had a very special good-luck charm: a "kinda crooked" long, red scarf that Raphael had given her.

The very same scarf he had been knitting during those long hours of training.